EGMONT

We bring stories to life

First published in Great Britain 2011 by Egmont UK Limited
239 Kensington High Street, London W8 6SA

Text copyright © Portobello Rights Limited 2011
Illustrations © Portobello Rights Limited and the BBC 2011,
taken from the BBC series 'World of Happy by Giles Andreae'
based on original illustrations by Janet Cronin

Giles Andreae has asserted his moral rights

A CIP catalogue record for this title is available from the British Library

ISBN 978 1 4052 5839 5
1 3 5 7 9 10 8 6 4 2
Printed in Italy

a story about being
BEAUTIFUL INSIDE

my name is ....

and things that make me happy are

....

....

....

There was once a hippopotamus . . .

who dreamed of being able to dance
with GRACE and BEAUTY.

However, when she tried, she could barely lift her BOTTOM off the ground and her stomach WOBBLED most uncomfortably indeed.

"It's just not fair,"
said the hippopotamus,
and she began to WEEP.

- ` sob ` -

- ` sniff ` -

"Come now," said a passing crocodile. "Perhaps you are simply trying the WRONG dance. What kind of dance would be YOUR dance – and YOUR dance ONLY?"

"Well, I am WALLOWY and BIG," sniffed the hippopotamus.

"I suppose I have never seen a dance of WALLOWY BIGNESS!"

Then she smiled.

"What a dance that would be!"

Slowly she began to move her hips.

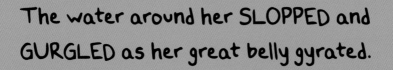

The water around her SLOPPED and GURGLED as her great belly gyrated.

And it felt GOOD.

She poured her whole HEART...

and SOUL into that dance.

And the music inside her rose to the surface . . .

like a silent ROAR...

A silent roar ....
of JOY.

fill yourself with

JOY
and
LOVELINESS

by visiting
worldofhappy.com

get the FREE app!

download fun stuff!

read all about the author!

world of happy